This book was initially inspired by all the hugs and affection we've missed
out on this past year, and it turned into an ode to all the wonderful ways
we can still love each other while we're apart.

It is dedicated to my beautiful Lebanon and its people.
We love you, near and far.
-R.M.

To little Ema,
I'll always love you, whether near or far.
-S.H.

I'll Love You from Afar
Text copyright © 2020 by Racha Mourtada
Illustrations copyright © 2020 by Sasha Haddad
All rights reserved. Manufactured in Italy.
For information address HarperCollins Children's Books, a division of HarperCollins Publishers,
195 Broadway, New York, NY 10007.
www.harpercollinschildrens.com

Library of Congress Control Number: 2021935333
ISBN 978-0-06-313888-9

Book design by Tanya Sawan
21 22 23 24 25   RTLO   10 9 8 7 6 5 4 3 2 1
❖
Originally published in 2020 by Luqoom

I'll Love You from Afar

Written by Racha Mourtada

Illustrated by Sasha Haddad

HARPER

An Imprint of HarperCollinsPublishers

Sorry I can't see you.
You're oh so far away!

But don't you worry,
I'm in no hurry,
My love is here to stay.

I miss your hugs and kisses
And all our silly games.
It's hardly as fun
On a seesaw for one.
Somehow, it's just not the same.

We may not be together,
But that's alright, you see.

The world is connected,
Our paths intersected,
If not now, eventually.

It's been a long time since I've felt
Your warm and ticklish touch.

I've been counting the days
And figuring out ways
To keep from missing you so much.

I'll travel underwater
In a small steel submarine

And tell the whales
To sing you tales
Of all the things I've seen!

I'll zoom off in a spaceship
On my way to Mars
And write you a note,
But my pencils would float,
So, instead, I'll spell it with stars!

I'll lie down in a meadow
On a sunny afternoon,
Send butterfly kisses
And dandelion wishes
Till the sun gives way to the moon.

And should the next day bring with it
Things scary or unexpected,
I will gather my might
And send love and light
So you'll always feel protected.

And if you're feeling down or blue,
And your problems seem quite large,

You can blow all your troubles
Into some bubbles,
And I'll pop them at no extra charge!

It doesn't matter where you are,
What place, what time of day.

If you're not near,
I'll still love you, dear,
My love won't fade away.

My love for you is everywhere,
In every little nook.

In birds that sing,
In the whisper of spring,
It's everywhere you look.

Until we meet again (real soon!),
I'll wish upon a star.

I'm in no race
For your embrace,
I'll love you from afar.